Bear Outside

Jane Yolen   Pictures by Jen Corace

NEAL PORTER BOOKS
HOLIDAY HOUSE / NEW YORK

For my daughter, Heidi, who has always worn her bear outside and is afraid of nothing. Thanks for taking care of your mom! —J.Y.

For Steven Malk —J.C.

Neal Porter Books

Text copyright © 2021 by Jane Yolen
Illustrations copyright © 2021 by Jen Corace
All Rights Reserved
HOLIDAY HOUSE is registered in the U.S. Patent and Trademark Office.
Printed and bound in November 2020 at Leo Paper, Heshan, China.
The artwork for this book was created using gouache, ink, and graphite
on Saunders Waterford watercolor paper.
Book design by Jennifer Browne
www.holidayhouse.com
First Edition
1 3 5 7 9 10 8 6 4 2

Library of Congress Cataloging-in-Publication Data

Names: Yolen, Jane, author. | Corace, Jen, illustrator.
Title: Bear outside / by Jane Yolen ; illustrated by Jen Corace.
Description: First edition. | New York : Holiday House, [2021] | "A Neal
Porter Book." | Audience: Ages 4 to 8. | Audience: Grades K–1. |
Summary: A little girl wears a bear on the outside to keep her safe and
to be her friend, just as some people have a fierce animal inside to
protect them.
Identifiers: LCCN 2020017365 | ISBN 9780823446131 (hardcover)
Subjects: CYAC: Courage—Fiction. | Self-confidence—Fiction. |
Bears—Fiction.
Classification: LCC PZ7.Y78 Bc 2021 | DDC [E]—dc23
LC record available at https://lccn.loc.gov/2020017365

ISBN 978-0-8234-4613-1 (hardcover)

Some folks have a lion inside,
or a tiger.
Not me.

I wear my bear on the outside.
It's like wearing a suit of armor.
She keeps out the howls,
the growls.
She keeps me safe.

I can wear my bear
anywhere—
schoolroom,

backyard,

grocery,

home.

I'm in charge,
riding my bike
to the stop sign.

Or if I like,
roller-skating.

Or bouncing
on the trampoline.

Bringing gifts
and favors
to our neighbors.

Only not at swimming lessons.
That can be dangerous
for both of us.

I take care
of Bear,
and Bear
takes care of me.

Together we find
the sweetest berries,
hives of honey,
to fatten me up.
We let the juices
run down our chins.

We're not afraid of bees
but buzz them back.
Then we nap beneath the trees.

At dinnertime,
we share a plate.
I like chicken,
Bear likes salad.

We don't always agree,
Bear and me.

When we do art projects,
Bear paints blue.
I use red.
Sometimes we make
purple instead.

At night we curl up
on the bed,
Bear on one side
me on the other.

Then mother reads us a story,
gives us kisses,
tucks us both in.

She says, "Good night, girls."
Leaves the night-light on.
Not for me,
I don't care.
I like the dark.

It's for Bear.